Rebecca Ventre

The Grouchy Mom

Illustrated by Darya Shchegoleva

Dedicated to my loves and inspiration Maya, Naomi, Cole and Cohen
Special thanks to Chris Ventre, Kat Penna, Gail Wilfred, Larry and Kay Smith

12/23

D0509100

Today, my mom woke up on the wrong side of the bed!
From the moment she got up,
SHE was GROUCHY!

At breakfast time mom made my favorite,
pancakes and eggs!

But before I could even take ONE bite,
I noticed that syrup was touching MY eggs!
And even though MY breakfast was ruined,
SHE was GROUCHY!

MY socks had lumps in them and MY shoes were too tight

and MY tag was itching me,
but for some reason
SHE was GROUCHY!

Then at snack time she told me
not to bring my drink to the carpet.
As I turned around to bring it back to the table,
it SPILLED!
And even though SHE told me to do it,
SHE was GROUCHY!

I tried to cheer her up
by drawing her a beautiful picture,
but it made her EVEN MORE GROUCHY!

Mom says baby brother is teething
and he has been fussing all day.
Maybe mom is getting a new tooth too!

At bath time I was BARELY splashing
and even though I only got a little water
on the floor, SHE was GROUCHY!

Dad called mom and said
he would be a little late coming home.
I was excited he would be home soon,
BUT it didn't help mom's mood at all!

At bedtime I was SO thirsty
and I wanted to hear ONE more story,
but mom seemed to be more
GROUCHY than EVER!

After she tucked me in,
I remembered what mom does to help me when I'm grouchy.
So, I called mom back to my room.

As she sat on my bed, I gave her a big hug
and told her how happy I am that she is my mommy.
She smiled and told me how much she loves me
as she kissed me goodnight.

I think she just needed some rest!

Made in the USA
Coppell, TX
21 May 2021